Printed in the United States of America

First Paperback Edition, January 2020

1 3 5 7 9 10 8 6 4 2

FAC-029261-19343

Library of Congress Control Number: 2019949225

ISBN: 978-1-368-05931-2

Visit disneybooks.com

SUSTAINABLE
FORESTRY
INITIATIVE
Certified Chain of Custody
Promoting Sustainable Forestry
www.sfiprogram.org
SFI-01054
The SFI label applies to the text stock

DISNEY
LADY AND THE TRAMP

JUNIOR NOVELIZATION

Adapted by Elizabeth Rudnick

Based on the Screenplay by
Andrew Bujalski and Kari Granlund

Produced by Brigham Taylor, p.g.a.

Directed by Charlie Bean

DISNEP PRESS

Los Angeles • New York

CHAPTER ONE

In the lovely little home Jim Dear and Darling called their own, the world was cozy, small, and safe. Their street was always quiet, the houses perfectly painted, the lawns well kept. Every morning, neighbors greeted Jim Dear with happy waves as he walked to retrieve his paper. Every evening, as he and his wife strolled down the tree-lined sidewalk, they heard the happy sounds of children playing or the occasional friendly bark of a dog. Not a thing was out of place. It was perfect.

Well, almost perfect.

One evening, as snow began to fall outside, Darling sat on the floor by a roaring fire. Over her, their Christmas tree sparkled and twinkled, the ornaments catching the firelight. Darling was happy. She loved her husband with all her heart. She loved their home and every piece of furniture and knickknack they had collected together. The end of the year and the holidays made her all the more grateful for everything she had. Sighing happily, she closed her eyes.

Hearing footsteps, Darling started to open them again.

"Keep them closed!" Jim Dear said. "Keep them closed. . . . Okay, you can open them."

Peeking with one eye, Darling cocked her head. Jim Dear held a hatbox. His usually pale cheeks were rosy from the cold, and his hair, typically brushed back off his face in the tidy style of the day, was messy. Her husband was a musician and had the soul of a poet, but he tried hard to look dapper.

"You think I need another hat?" she asked playfully.

Jim Dear shook his head. Gently, he placed the hatbox on the floor. "Guess again," he said.

Just then, the box moved and made a rustling sound. Darling sat up straighter, her eyes widening. She got to her knees and carefully removed the lid from the box. Brushing away a layer of soft tissue paper, she let out a happy squeal as two big brown eyes appeared. It was a puppy! Darling reached in and lifted the puppy from the box. The cocker spaniel was adorable, with long, wavy brown ears and a brown-and-white body. She wiggled excitedly in Darling's hands.

"Well, Darling?"

Darling looked up at her husband and then back down at the puppy. "She's perfect," Darling cooed. "A perfect little lady."

At the word, the puppy's tail wagged even faster. Lady had found a home.

When Lady had been put in the hatbox, it had scared her at first. But as soon as she had locked eyes with the kind woman who had opened it, she had felt safe—and loved. For the rest of the evening, she sat in the woman's lap while the woman—who smelled of lavender and honey—gently rubbed Lady's belly and gave her kisses. Lady had discovered that her new humans were named Darling and Jim Dear and that they loved each other—and her—very, very much.

Only now Darling and Jim Dear seemed to be leaving her. The moon had come out and the stars were twinkling in the sky, so Lady knew it was night. But she wasn't sure why that meant she had to leave her new family. As they put a big dog bed down in the middle of the pantry, Lady wiggled in Darling's arms.

"There, there, Lady," Darling said. Lady knew she was trying to make her feel better, but she didn't like the looks of the pantry door.

A moment later, Jim Dear put a few pieces of newspaper down and gave her a pat on the head, and then they turned and left. The door shut behind them.

Lady was alone.

She stood still for a moment, looking from the bed to the newspaper to the heavy door. Letting out a little yip, she rushed at the paper and grabbed it between her teeth, shaking it. A puppy growl formed in the back of her throat. The noise she made startled her, and Lady dropped the paper.

She moved to the door and shoved her nose against it. It didn't budge. She pushed again. This time the door swung a little bit. She pushed again and again until the door swung wide enough that she could slip through, out of the pantry. Wandering the house, she sniffed and nosed a pair of shoes on the floor. She hopped over a guitar, then finally, she made it to the stairs.

Lady looked up. The stairs were long. She hadn't noticed that before. But she had to get up them. At the top were Darling and Jim Dear.

Taking a deep breath, Lady put both her front paws on the bottom stair. Then she pushed off with her back paws. She hung for a moment and then fell back to the floor. She wagged her puppy tail and tried again. She made it! Step by step, Lady worked her way to the top. By the time she reached the landing, she was out of breath.

She had not been upstairs before. The hallway was dark and narrow, with several doors. Putting her nose to the ground, Lady followed the smell of lavender. Walking through an open door, she saw Darling and Jim Dear asleep on a bed. She made her way to it and jumped up, then flopped down on Darling's stomach.

Murmuring, Darling rolled over, the movement landing Lady right atop Jim Dear's face. Startled, the man woke up. Seeing Lady, he sighed. But he did not, as she'd feared, take her back downstairs. Instead, he arranged a makeshift bed on the floor. He placed her down on it and crawled back into bed.

Lady waited a moment, then jumped off her bed and back onto the humans' bed. It was much more comfortable. Darling wrapped her arms around Lady and pulled her close.

Next to her, Jim Dear sighed again. "All right," he said, his voice heavy with sleep. "Just for one night."

Lady wiggled happily, pushing her body as close to Darling as she could. She closed her eyes. She didn't know what a Christmas miracle was, exactly, but Darling had called her one several times. Whatever it was, she was glad she was one.

Lady's one night turned into two. And then two more and then two more. Soon six months had passed, and Lady was as much at home in the bed and house as Jim Dear and Darling.

Her life had taken on a lovely routine. In the morning she collected the paper from the end of the walk and promptly returned it to Darling. After a quick breakfast, Lady and Jim Dear took a stroll down the tree-lined street. If Jim Dear happened to forget, Lady had no problem reminding him. Leash in her mouth, she gave a quick bark and a wag of her tail, and Jim Dear was on his feet and heading for the door.

Afternoons were spent exploring the yard. There was always something to see—a butterfly floating through the air in a zigzag pattern, a newly blossomed flower. Most days Jim Dear took time to bring her a small round ball, which he threw to her endlessly. She loved that game—especially because whenever she brought the ball back, she got a happy "good girl, Lady." Those were some of her favorite words.

When evening came around and dinner was over, she, Darling, and Jim Dear curled up on the couch together while the humans read or listened to the radio. Lady fell asleep to Darling's gentle touch as she gave her belly rubs, and to the sound of Darling's soft voice as she told Jim Dear about her day.

Life was perfect, just the three of them, with each of Lady's days better than the last.

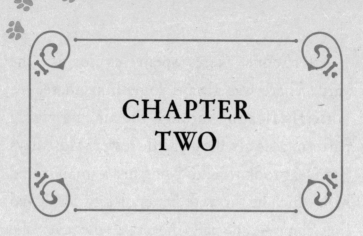

CHAPTER TWO

"Have you ever seen such a perfect dog?"

Lady sat in front of a long mirror, staring at her reflection. Behind her, Darling knelt down, a thin piece of leather in her hand.

"No, I certainly haven't," Jim Dear replied.

Lady wagged her tail. But when she looked up, she saw that Jim Dear wasn't looking at her; he was looking at his wife. Lady smiled. Her humans loved each other so much.

Returning Jim's smile, Darling reached over and gently placed the leather collar around Lady's neck. Lady had been waiting for an official collar ever since she arrived at her new home. She had been too small before, but now that she was nearly grown, it was time. The collar was perfect—thin and delicate, just right for her little body. Lady's eyes widened as she saw what was dangling from it: a small gold heart. Across the heart, "Lady" was written in elegant script.

Lady had never before seen anything quite as beautiful. Her tail wagged and her backside nearly lifted off the ground. She was too excited to sit still!

Sensing the dog's eagerness, Darling smiled and gave Lady a quick pat on the head. "Why don't you go show Jock and Trusty?" she said.

Lady didn't need to be told twice. She leaped up and raced out of the room, through the doggy door in the kitchen, and out toward the backyard. Her steps slowed as she approached the back porch. Milk and eggs from the day's delivery were splattered across the wood. Lady's eyes narrowed. Putting her nose to the ground, she began to sniff, trying to figure out who had done such a thing. Then she saw them: footprints. And not just any footprints! The rat was back.

Following the prints along the side of the house, she kept her eyes peeled. Just as she arrived at the end of the porch, she spotted the rat. Its beady eyes stared back at her, and then, baring its teeth and hissing, it leaped off the porch and raced across the lawn toward the fence that separated Lady's yard from the neighbors'.

Lady barked and gave chase. Reaching the fence, the ugly little creature dove through a hole and disappeared on the other side. Lady barked one last time, and then, satisfied with her job of protecting her house, she turned and trotted toward the front yard.

Lying on his porch next door, taking a long afternoon nap, was Trusty. The bloodhound was old, his red coat flecked with gray, his drooping ears no longer as keen as they had once been. But he was one of Lady's best friends, and she adored him.

"Trusty! Guess what!" Lady said, walking toward him. Without the humans around, she and her friends could talk openly. "I just came so close to catching the rat. You should've seen it!"

"Rat?" Trusty said, waking with a start. He looked around for a moment, his eyes heavy. "Where?" Lifting his nose in the air, he took a big sniff. Then he struggled to his feet and made his way off the porch, following a scent he clearly couldn't find.

Lady laughed. Trusty's days of being a police dog were long over, but that didn't stop him from thinking he was at the top of his game. "No, no, no," she said. "It's gone. I just gave it a good scare."

The older dog relaxed. "Ah, well done," he said with a nod of his big head. "Haven't smelled one of those vile vermin in a while. Reminds me of my early days on the force. Barely grown into my paws—"

"Trusty," Lady interrupted. She knew what would happen if he started down memory lane. "You think you can sniff out what's different about *me* today?" To give him a clue, she lifted her chin so that her neck was more exposed. Then she shook her head, causing the tag to twinkle.

The bloodhound was immediately on the alert. "Detective work!" he said happily. "My specialty. I may be retired, but ol' reliable here sure ain't." He gestured to his nose. Trusty moved closer to Lady. He sniffed the top of her head, her ears, even her neck. But he clearly didn't pick up the scent.

"New collar!" someone called out.

Turning, Lady saw her friend Jock coming from the other side of the lawn. The Scottish terrier was, as usual, dressed up. Jock's human loved to put the little black dog in outfits and then take her portrait. That day she wore an argyle sweater.

Prancing over, Jock nodded at Lady's neck. "A gold heart," she said. She sounded impressed. "Must mean they really love you. They want to show you off on walks. Make way for Lady, walking royalty."

"I'm hardly royalty," Lady protested weakly. Darling and Jim Dear *did* treat her very well.

Trusty stepped closer and jingled the tag. "That there's a badge of honor," he said in his slow, deep voice. "Not like my actual badge of honor from the boys in blue." His eyes glazed over as he began to tell Lady and Jock a story about his early days on the force. Lady and Jock shared a look. They had heard this one before—many, *many* times. But neither of them had the heart to tell Trusty to stop.

When his story was finally over, Trusty sniffed the air. "You smell that?" he asked. "I reckon that infernal rat may be back. I'll secure the perimeter. Y'all stay here where it's safe." Orders given, Trusty ambled off.

Just then, Stephanie, Jock's human, walked out onto the porch of her house. She held a black-and-white striped shirt and a doggy beret. "I've gotta go," Jock said. "It's portrait time!" She started to trot off but stopped and looked back at Lady. "Congrats on the collar. Seems like your family's just about perfect."

Lady nodded. Jock was right. Her family really *was* perfect.

Nothing could ruin that.

But later that night, as Lady sat on the couch between Darling and Jim Dear, she noticed something strange. When Darling said, "This is nice," which was what she usually said as they sat together, Jim Dear didn't pet Lady, which was what he usually did when Darling said that. Instead, he reached over and gently placed his hand on Darling's stomach.

"It sure is," he answered. Lady watched, confused. His hand didn't leave Darling's stomach, which Lady suddenly noticed seemed a bit larger than usual.

What could that mean? Lady wondered.

CHAPTER THREE

In the train yard, things were bustling. Trains hissed with steam, and brakes screeched. As workers shoveled coal into the beds of various train cars, dark soot lifted into the air. A bit farther down the yard, men slammed large hammers onto metal, shaping it into rails. It was noisy, dirty, and hot—a far cry from the peace and quiet of the tree-lined street where Lady lived.

In an abandoned train car in the middle of the yard, Tramp slept, not bothered by the noise or the trash that lined the floor. Tramp was considered a mutt—a mix of different dog breeds—and this was his home. He lived wild and free—no collar to keep him restrained, no family to keep him trapped.

Getting to his feet, Tramp stretched and let out a big yawn. He shook his shaggy gray coat and gave his ear a scratch. "Isn't this the life?" he said to himself, genuinely happy.

"Hey! No trespassing!"

Hearing the loud, angry voice, Tramp looked toward the open door of the train car. A moment later the foreman's face appeared. He pulled himself into the car.

As the foreman stomped toward him, Tramp dodged out of the way. "Guess we're starting early today," he said to himself as he slipped out the door. Behind him, he heard muttering from the foreman and then the crunch of rocks as the big man jumped out of the car and gave chase.

Tramp didn't run out of fear. His stride stayed even. He had done this song and dance with the foreman before. It was almost a game at this point—like the game of fetch dogs with families played with their owners. Only in this case, Tramp was the ball and he was trying *not* to get caught.

Leaping over a rail and through a train car, Tramp easily made his way through the yard. He knew where the best hiding spots were and which paths to take to avoid the unfriendly foreman. After years of making the train yard his home base, he was considered a local to the various workers, too.

Now, as he passed by a line of welders, masks down over their faces, he heard several of them call out in greeting. "Check it out! It's Buddy!" one of them said.

"Better speed up, pal," another said, nodding at the foreman, who was gaining on the dog.

Tramp picked up speed. He still wasn't worried. He leaped over a thin trough and landed lightly on a narrow set of rails. Behind him he heard a splash and a shout as the foreman tried to follow and ended up falling in the muddy water next to the rails instead.

Looking back, Tramp saw the stuck foreman. With a wag of his tail, Tramp turned and sauntered out of the train yard. The workers hooted and hollered. It didn't matter how many mornings Tramp outsmarted the foreman; it made them smile every time. To the workers in the train yard, he was a hero.

As Tramp made his way along the outskirts of the town, the sounds and smells of the train yard faded. He passed the docks, busy with workers preparing the riverboats that would cruise passengers up and down the shore, entertaining them with jazz music and plying them with delicious feasts. Workers waved and shouted hello. Tramp was a familiar sight everywhere he walked.

Soon the gentle breeze from the river disappeared as Tramp entered the busier streets and alleys that made up the city center. Tramp didn't like it there. Downtown meant more people, and that meant more people who might complain about a stray dog— which meant dogcatchers. And Tramp *hated* dogcatchers.

Peering around a corner, Tramp scanned the square in front of him for any signs of danger. Spotting none, he slipped down the sidewalk and into the nearest alley. The dark, narrow space seemed empty. But Tramp knew better than to take any chances. This was Isaac's alley. "Isaac?" Tramp called out. "Isaac! You here?" When no one responded, Tramp trotted farther into the alley.

Following his nose, he made his way to

a huge trash can. It was overflowing with delicious treasure—old bones, leftover food, sausage links. Tramp's stomach growled. Jumping up, he grabbed a link of sausages in his mouth. He was just about to bite down when a low growl echoed through the alley.

Tramp froze.

"Get your paws off my stuff."

Slowly, Tramp turned around. Towering behind him was Isaac. The brawny dog's lips were curled up, revealing sharp teeth. Tramp let the sausage drop from his mouth as he took a few steps back. "Isaac!" he said, laying on the charm. "I was just looking for you. How are you, my big, sweet, kind, pugnacious friend?"

"Do I look like a pug to you?" Isaac snarled.

Tramp bit back a laugh. "No—I . . ." He started to explain and then thought better of it. "Never mind." The big dog's brains did not match his body.

Puffing up his chest, Isaac stalked closer to Tramp. There were two things Isaac hated—being made fun of and having his stuff taken. Right then, Tramp seemed to be doing both, and Isaac did not like it one bit.

"Someone has been stealing from my stash," he said. "Should have known it would be a dirty tramp like you."

Tramp put on his most innocent face. "You think I was stealing? C'mon, Isaac, I'm no thief!"

Isaac eyed the sausages. "Then what are you doing with those?"

Looking down at the string of sausages at his feet, Tramp hesitated. The last thing he wanted was to have Isaac after him for the rest of the day. *Think, think,* Tramp chanted to himself in his head. Then he smiled. That was it! He just had to *outthink* Isaac. That couldn't be too hard.

Taking a deep breath, as if he had just had a great revelation, Tramp tapped the sausages. "Oh! I see what happened!" he said. "No, see, these are *my* sausages."

Isaac cocked his head. "What?" He was clearly confused—which was just how Tramp wanted him.

"I heard someone was lifting your stuff," Tramp went on. He lowered his voice and added, as though it were a secret, "A lot of the dogs are talking about it."

There was something Isaac hated even more than having his stuff stolen and being made fun of, and that was other dogs talking about him behind his back. "Who's talking?" he growled.

Tramp pushed ahead, mentioning quickly— very quickly—that he had, of course, not wanted Isaac to go hungry or be made a fool of because his sausages were being taken. So out of the kindness of his heart, he had brought his *own* sausages to share.

"Share?" Isaac asked.

Tramp nodded. "How does half sound?"

Isaac shook his head. "Nice try, smart guy," he said, "but I'm going to take a lot more than half your sausages."

"How about sixty–forty?" Tramp said as though it were really kind of him even to offer that. In reality, he was still winning out.

"Seventy–forty," Isaac countered.

Tramp pretended to give in. He pushed just slightly more than half toward Isaac, then gathered the rest of the sausages for himself. "Serves me right, trying to match wits with you. You just talked me out of half my sausages."

Eager to get out while the getting was good, Tramp headed out of the alley. Another narrow escape. The morning really was off to a good start.

CHAPTER FOUR

The rest of the morning was more of the same. Stopping by the park, Tramp eyed a gentleman sitting on one of the many benches that lined the paths. A sandwich was placed on a piece of parchment paper beside him. Tramp's mouth watered. The sausages had been tasty, but Tramp was always up for a bite. While the owner was distracted, Tramp nabbed the sandwich. Trotting away, he had only made it to the other corner of the park before he lost his snack. Two stray puppies, eyes wide and ribs showing, stared up at him—or, rather, at his sandwich.

"Come on," Tramp said. "Don't give me that look."

But it was no use. He didn't have the heart to say no—even if he had invented that look. Tossing the pups his sandwich, Tramp continued on his way. This was a wandering day. It was beautiful—sunny, not too hot, not too cold. He made his way along River Street, then turned down another alley behind Restaurant Row. This was his favorite spot in the city. The alley was a treasure trove of leftover food. Tramp could sample French cuisine or have some good old-fashioned American fare. But his favorite was Tony's Restaurant. There was always something tasty waiting for him behind the Italian restaurant.

Approaching the back door of the restaurant, Tramp spotted Joe. The young man had been working at the restaurant for as long as Tramp could remember. Tramp barked, and Joe looked up from scraping leftovers and smiled. He grabbed a large meaty bone and held it up. "Here you go, Butch," he said, tossing the bone to Tramp.

Tramp grabbed the bone in one swift and easy move. Then, with a bark of thanks and a wag of his tail, he moved along. There was no doubt about it: Tramp ran this town.

Not everyone agreed that Tramp was the king of the town. In fact, the local dogcatcher, Elliott, thought Tramp was nothing but trouble.

Spotting the dogcatcher standing in front of a store window, Tramp ducked into the shadows. Elliott's brow was furrowed as he taped a piece of paper to the glass. Stepping back, he admired his handiwork. On the paper were several pictures of dogs and a number to call if a stray was spotted. Tramp made out the word "dangerous." He laughed. That was a bit ridiculous. The most dangerous thing he knew was Elliott—not the dogs he pulled off the street.

Careful to stay out of sight, Tramp made his way across the street to Elliott's parked paddy wagon. The big vehicle looked innocent enough—until you got close and saw the bars on the back and heard the whimpers of captured animals coming from inside.

"Hiya, handsome," someone said from inside the truck.

Tiptoeing over, Tramp saw his pals Peg and Bull. The Lhasa apso and the rough-and-tumble bulldog were staring at him through the bars. "C'mon," Tramp said, moving closer. "What happened?" The pair had been on the street as long as he had. They knew better than to get caught.

Bull shrugged his thick shoulders. "I had the idea to summer at the pound. Get off the streets for a bit, rest the rump . . ." He stopped. "What does it look like? We got caught!"

Beside him, Peg began to groom herself, trying to get her usually tamed coat back into some order. The fur was going every which way. Peg prided herself on always looking good. She was probably more upset about her coat than being stuck in the truck. "Some nerve of that guy," Peg said, confirming Tramp's thoughts about Elliott. "You think this hair styles itself?"

Tramp shook his head. "You guys make it too easy on him when you hang together," he whispered. Peg and Bull, while an unlikely pair, were helplessly attached to each other. That was not Tramp's style.

"We can't all play lone wolf," Peg replied, as if reading Tramp's thoughts.

"I'm sorry. Was that a compliment?" Tramp teased, flashing Peg a charming smile. "Because I don't mind the way 'wolf' sounds."

Peg wasn't biting. She knew Tramp's act, and she didn't have time for it that day. She needed him to get them out. Lucky for her, Tramp was feeling up for a challenge.

He paced back and forth in front of the truck, trying to think of a plan. He needed something that would get Elliott's attention but leave him with a way out. The last thing he wanted was to free Peg and Bull and end up captured himself. Finally, he settled on a plan that was an oldie but a goodie.

He dropped to the ground and lay down. Then he began to whimper. By the store window, Elliott's head snapped to attention. Elliott moved across the street, walked around the truck, and spotted Tramp.

"C'mon, at least give me a challenge." He

got closer and knelt down. When Tramp didn't make a move to get away, Elliott smiled. He slipped his arms under Tramp and lifted him.

Instantly, Tramp went limp, causing Elliott's legs to buckle. The man groaned as he struggled under Tramp's weight. Tramp made himself even limper. Elliott awkwardly moved closer to the back door of the truck. He unlocked the door—just as Tramp leaped from his arms and darted across the street.

Elliott shouted in surprise. He looked from his now empty arms to the dog, who no longer seemed hurt at all. His eyes narrowed. The dog had tricked him.

Pleased with his successful distraction, Tramp wagged his tail, then turned and took off down the street. Behind him, he heard Elliott muttering to himself as he grabbed his net and followed Tramp.

The chase was on.

Just like in the train yard, Tramp had the advantage. He knew the streets better than Elliott—better than anyone. Spotting a passing trolley car, Tramp leaped into it and dodged and weaved his way among the passengers' legs. Elliott followed. But the man's bulky frame made it hard for him to move quickly. Men and women let out angry cries as they were pushed out of the way.

"Clear a path," Elliott said. "Animal control officer coming through."

No one moved—except Tramp.

Making his way to the other end of the trolley, Tramp looked over his shoulder. Elliott's eyes landed on him. They narrowed. Tramp barked once and then jumped from the trolley car onto the back of a passing delivery truck.

As the truck continued on, the driver was unaware of his new passenger. Tramp glanced back at the trolley car. Elliott stood in the doorway, his hand raised in the air, his face a mask of anger. Tramp smiled. Now he just had to hope the distraction had given Peg and Bull time to get away.

He lay down and closed his eyes as the truck headed into the nice part of town. He would take a quick nap. It had been a busy morning.

CHAPTER FIVE

Lady was confused. Her house was full of people, but none of them were paying attention to her. Pink and blue balloons floated above the dining room table, which was covered in food—cupcakes, little sandwiches, and fruit. The living room was full of presents, and women giggled and chatted with each other.

At the top of the stairs, Lady stood and watched, leash in her mouth. She had been waiting forever for Jim Dear to take her on their morning walk. Every time he passed by, Lady wagged her tail excitedly and jingled the leash. But he didn't notice. He kept tugging nervously at his suit, and his face was pale. So why didn't he take her on a walk? Lady wondered. It would make them both feel better.

Lady ran down the stairs and headed toward the living room. Maybe Darling would take her out. But when she walked into the room, she saw that Darling, whose belly had grown quite large, was sitting on the couch, surrounded by women.

Walking over, Lady tried to get Darling's attention. It was hard. Darling was surrounded by blue and pink and yellow packages. "Oh, my goodness!" Darling said happily. "It's adorable."

Assuming Darling meant her, Lady looked up happily. But her smile faded as she saw that Darling was talking about a small stuffed bear, not her. She gingerly stepped between the presents, trying to get closer. She had almost made it to Darling's side when she heard a commotion at the door.

A moment later, Aunt Sarah waltzed in. Lady had met Aunt Sarah only once. But she didn't like her. The woman smelled like cat, and she spoke fast and loudly. From the look on Darling's face, she could tell her human wasn't thrilled to see Aunt Sarah, either.

"Aunt Sarah," Darling said. "You made it."

Aunt Sarah pushed her way through the other women to get to Darling. She leaned down and gave Darling a kiss on each cheek before plopping herself onto the couch. Another woman who had been sitting there was forced to move.

"Of course," Aunt Sarah said. She paused, looking around the room. "Your house is very . . . modern. Don't worry, it takes time to develop an eye for these things." Lady didn't like the tone of Aunt Sarah's voice. She sounded unimpressed. Lady loved her house and knew Darling did, too. Before Darling could respond, Aunt Sarah shoved a present at her. "This is for you."

Darling carefully unwrapped the present. She lifted the object out of the wrapping. Lady cocked her head. It was a big vase.

"Oh, wow," Darling said, "it's an—"

"Original majolica," Aunt Sarah finished, looking incredibly pleased with herself. "It'll do wonders for this room. And I knew Jim couldn't afford one with the salary of a—"

"Musician?" Darling finished. On the floor, Lady tensed. Darling seemed upset. Wanting to comfort her, Lady moved closer and then hopped up onto the couch. The movement nearly knocked the vase out of Darling's hands.

"Careful! This is priceless!" Aunt Sarah snapped as Lady tried to make herself comfortable. "That dog needs to be trained."

Expecting Darling to come to her defense—Lady was very well trained—she was surprised when Darling picked her up and put her back on the floor. "Not now, Lady," she said.

Lady walked away, embarrassed. First Jim wouldn't give her a walk. Now Darling acted like she wanted nothing to do with her. What was going on?

Since no one seemed to want her around, Lady decided to go outside. Maybe Trusty or Jock would be home and could explain why everyone was acting so funny. Slipping through the doggy door, Lady made her way to the vine-covered fence. On the other side she heard a rustling noise. Trusty must be sniffing for something. "Hey, Trusty," she called out.

The big bloodhound didn't respond. But Lady went on anyway. "Something strange is going on," she began. "There's a bunch of toys, and none of them are for me. And I just jumped onto Darling's lap like I always do, but this time . . . she snapped at me." Lady paused. Saying the words out loud made her feel terrible all over again. "And Jim Dear? Well, he *seems* normal, but I smell fear on him all the time." She paused, waiting for Trusty to say something. He was quiet. "I'm overreacting, aren't I?"

"Uh, no. You aren't overreacting."

Lady's head snapped up. That wasn't Trusty's voice! As she peered through a hole in the fence, her eyes widened. On the other side was a dog she had never seen before. He was a mutt with big brown eyes and a rough coat. One of his ears flopped down, giving him a playful look. He was handsome, in a rough-and-tumble way, Lady thought. Then she shook her head. Why was she thinking about him being handsome? He had just eavesdropped on her private—well, sort of private—thoughts.

"Who are you?" she asked. "Where's Trusty?"

The dog scrambled up and over the fence, then landed on the ground in front of Lady. He gave her a charming grin. "Let me explain . . ." he said.

Lady didn't let him finish. She began to bark.

"Easy, easy," Tramp said, holding up a paw to calm down the dog in front of him.

When he had woken up in the back of the delivery truck miles from downtown, he hadn't been worried. He had figured he would just take a leisurely walk home, look at some nice houses. He hadn't expected to get distracted by a pretty little dog with a barking problem.

"You're overreacting," he said. If she kept it up, Elliott, who was probably still looking for him, would find him. "Could you please stop overreacting?"

Hearing Elliott's paddy wagon coming down the street, Tramp shifted nervously on his feet. He needed the dog to stop barking— now. "I get it," he said, trying to keep his voice calm. "You think I'm here to *make* trouble. I'm the one *in* trouble."

As if on cue, Elliott's net poked into view.

At the same time, the back door to the house opened and a man's head popped out. Quickly, Tramp scrambled backward, wedging his lanky body into the doghouse.

"Everything all right, Lady?" the man called out to the pretty cocker spaniel staring daggers at Tramp.

Lady gave a bark.

"That your dog barking?" the dogcatcher

asked. Tramp saw Elliott walking around from the other side of the fence. The man's beady little eyes were narrowed as they scanned the lawn.

"Yeah, she's mine," the man answered.

Elliott frowned. "Seen anything else? I'm looking for a dangerous animal around here."

Inside the doghouse, Tramp bit back a laugh. The man on the porch seemed to find the statement funny, too. He made a face. "Like a bear?" he asked, clearly teasing the dogcatcher.

Elliott missed the sarcasm. "Worse," he said very seriously. "A stray dog."

The man walked down the steps of the porch and over to Lady. "You barking at a stray, Lady?"

For one long moment, Tramp was sure Lady was going to tell on him. He looked at her, his eyes wide, begging her silently to keep him safe. Finally, she wagged her tail. Taking that as a no, the man turned back to the dogcatcher. "Nope," he said. "Everything seems to be fine." Giving Lady a pat on the head, the man began to usher the dogcatcher out of the yard.

The backyard grew quiet.

Tramp squeezed himself out of the doghouse and approached Lady. "Thanks," he said. "I owe you one."

Lady looked at him. She did not seem impressed. "You owe me more than one, I'd say."

Tramp shrugged. She was probably right. With the danger gone, he could finally take a serious look around the yard. It was neat and clean, the grass green and the porch cozy. His eyes stopped on a stroller by the back door. He remembered Lady's words. "First baby, huh?" he said, nodding at the stroller.

"First . . . what?" Lady asked. She looked confused and worried.

Tramp felt oddly sorry for her. She seemed like a sweet dog. She had no way to know her life was about to be rocked. Tramp sat down. "You're the center of your people's universe, right?" he asked. Lady nodded. "They make you feel special and loved every day?"

Again, Lady nodded. "Every day."

"Well, that's all over now," Tramp said. "You're about to be replaced."

"Replaced?" Lady repeated. Then she shook her head. "You don't know what you're talking about."

"Look, kid," he said with a shrug, "I know people. People aren't loyal. My philosophy? Look out for yourself. The sooner you start doing that, the better."

Suddenly, two other dogs rushed into the yard. Tramp looked up, surprised. Then he relaxed. It was an old bloodhound and a little

Scottish terrier wearing . . . a hat and a scarf?

"Lady! Are you okay? Stay back, mongrel!" the terrier said.

"Just gimme a reason, stray," the old bloodhound said in a gravelly voice.

"Better not give him that reason, mangy mongrel," Jock added.

Tramp almost laughed. It was hard to take a threat seriously when the dog doing the threatening was dressed up. "Keep your scarf on, killer," he said.

Then Lady spoke. "It's okay," she said to her friends. "He was just leaving. Weren't you . . . street dog?"

Tramp sighed. And there it was: the stereotype. Lady was just like every other dog—and human—he had met. Always assuming he was nothing but trouble. All he had been doing was trying to help her, give her a heads-up.

Turning to go, Tramp looked over his

shoulder. "Just remember," he said, "when a baby moves in, the dog moves out." He began to trot away, but not before grabbing a bone that was lying in the grass. "I'm stealing this, by the way," he said. Then, with a wink, he was off.

He had tried to do her a favor. He had warned her about what was to come. If she didn't want to hear it, that was her problem. He had a bone to chew on, and Elliott was off his back. He was good to go. Lady was going to have to figure out her life on her own.

CHAPTER SIX

Something was different. Lady felt it—and smelled it. The house still looked the same. The front porch was still as lovely, the white latticework as bright as always against the cream-colored siding. The inside was still picture perfect, the rooms still cozy and the wallpaper—covered with birds and flowers— still cheerful. But somehow, while everything was the same, it had completely changed.

The baby had arrived.

Lying on her dog bed in the living room, Lady listened as Darling sang a lullaby to

Lulu. The sound was soothing. Curious, Lady got up and quietly went up the stairs and to the door of the nursery. She peeked inside. Darling's back was to Lady. She was rocking slowly back and forth, her long white gown shifting in the gentle breeze that blew from the window. Lady tried to get a glimpse of Lulu, but all she could see was a blanket. She gave a little yip to say hello.

Jim Dear, who had been standing by the crib, jumped at the noise. He rushed to the door. "Shhh," he whispered. He leaned down and ushered Lady from the doorway. "Sorry, girl, not now."

Sadly, Lady turned and walked along the hall. Through the window in Darling and Jim Dear's room she could look down at Trusty's house. She saw Trusty and his person eating at a table together in the kitchen. Trusty's human still wanted *him* around. She continued down the stairs. Pausing at a window, she glanced at Jock's house. The Scottish terrier was sitting on a stool while her human, Stephanie, took photographs of her. Finishing up, Stephanie clapped her hands and opened her arms for a hug. Jock leaped off the stool and ran to her. Stephanie still wanted Jock around.

But Darling and Jim Dear didn't want Lady around at all. They only wanted Lulu.

Sighing, Lady walked down the rest of the stairs and into the living room. But as she headed for her bed, she heard a scratching noise by the living room window. Her ears perked up. As she looked at the window, the hair on her neck rose. Staring back at her was a pair of beady little eyes. The rat! It was back. Lady raced to the window, jumped up on her hind legs, and rested her paws on the windowsill. A low growl rose in her throat, and then she let out a bark.

The rat scampered away. But Lady kept barking. Hearing the sound of Jim Dear's footsteps on the stairs, Lady turned, expecting him to look happy for her good protecting. Instead, he looked angry.

Confused, she let him pick her up and carry her through the house and out the back door of the kitchen. Placing her down on the back porch, Jim Dear shook his head. Then, without a word, he went back inside, leaving Lady alone.

Lady plopped down. "When the baby moves in, the dog moves out," she said softly to herself. She didn't want to admit it, but that stray dog might have been right.

—

The next few weeks, Lady found herself spending more and more time outside. She was still allowed to sleep on her bed in the living room. But she no longer got to cuddle with Jim Dear and Darling. Lulu got that spot. And long walks were over. If she was lucky, Jim Dear would take her for a quick walk down to the end of the street and back. She was beginning to think things couldn't get worse.

And then Jim Dear and Darling packed their suitcase.

And the next day, Aunt Sarah arrived.

She burst into the house, a bag in her hand. Setting it on the hall floor, she moved inside as if she owned the place. Coming down to greet her, Darling held Lulu in her arms.

"Thank you so much for watching Lady while we're gone," she said, giving her aunt a quick kiss on the cheek.

"Just dog sitting?" Aunt Sarah said, clearly not pleased by the news. "I thought I'd be in the company of little Lulu."

Ignoring the woman's comment, Jim Dear gave her a strained smile. He turned from Aunt Sarah, walked over to Lady, and knelt down. Giving her a quick pat on the head, he added, "Bye, Lady."

And then, just like that, they headed out the door. It shut behind them with a dull thud.

Lady raced to the window and watched as her people—her whole world—got into their Model T and drove down the street. "Don't leave me," she whispered. But it was too late. The car had already turned a corner and disappeared from view.

Lady was alone with Aunt Sarah.

Backing up so she was on the opposite side of the room, Lady watched as Aunt Sarah picked up her suitcase and headed upstairs. Aunt Sarah left behind a large basket, which, as Lady looked on, began to move. Curious, Lady walked over just as the lid on the basket popped open. A moment later, two pairs of eyes peered over the edge, and then, to Lady's horror, a pair of identical cats slithered out. Lady quickly backed away as Devon and Rex moved into the room. They smiled slyly as they crisscrossed in front of each other, their steps in perfect unison.

"Ew . . ." began Devon, "this couldn't be our . . ."

"New home," finished Rex. He looked disgusted.

"Not much space to stretch . . ." Devon went on.

"Our legs," Rex once again finished.

Ignoring Lady, the cats stopped, and then their lips pulled back over their teeth. Rex continued, "But I think we could make some . . ."

In unison, they hissed, "Changesss. . . ."

Lady cringed. That didn't sound good. Then,

as she watched, the cats began to destroy the living room. Devon jumped onto the couch and dug his claws into it. There was a ripping sound as the fabric tore. Rex went to the mantel. His eyes moved up and down the dark wood, stopping at the collection of knickknacks and dolls Darling had carefully put on the shelf. He leaped up smoothly and began to weave around the objects. Lady's breath caught. He was going to knock them over!

"Be careful!" she warned.

But Rex didn't hear her—or didn't care. Lifting his paw, he swiped a porcelain figurine off the shelf. It fell to the floor, shattering into dozens of pieces. Helpless to do anything, Lady watched as the cats continued to move around the room. They ripped up the carpet and shredded the lovely curtains Darling had made. They tore at the wallpaper and clawed at the floors.

Lady had had enough.

Letting out a growl, she took off after the cats. She chased them into the dining room. Both cats jumped onto the long table, their claws digging into the wood. As Devon slammed into a vase, spilling flowers and water everywhere, Rex jumped onto the antique cuckoo clock. Trying to shove his large body into the small window of the clock, he managed to break the bird that announced the hour. A moment later, the whole clock fell.

Their job in that room done, the cats headed into the kitchen. Lady winced as she heard plates and glasses breaking. She faintly heard Aunt Sarah call out her name upstairs. But she didn't pay attention. Her focus was on the cats. Careering out of the kitchen, they raced by her and back toward the living room. Lady followed. But just as they got to the fireplace, the cats veered off in separate directions. Lady didn't have time to slow down. With a cry, she flew into the fireplace, sending ash shooting up into the air.

Coughing and sneezing, Lady emerged from the fireplace. She looked up and froze. Rex and Devon were perched on top of the china cabinet. Inside, placed in the middle of all the other pieces, was the majolica vase Aunt Sarah had given Darling.

In horror, Lady watched as the cats began to rock back and forth. The cabinet began to move. Then, with a groan, it fell. As the china crashed down, the majolica fell and, miraculously, landed safely on a chair. But then it started to roll to the edge. Lady rushed over and lifted her nose, stopping the vase just before it fell. She let out a sigh of relief.

"Lady!"

Startled by the sound, Lady turned. Aunt Sarah stood in the doorway, her hands on her hips, fury in her eyes. The vase, without Lady's nose to keep it stable, toppled to the ground. As Aunt Sarah screamed out, "My majolica," the precious object shattered into a thousand pieces.

Lady lowered her head.

She was in trouble. Big, big trouble.

CHAPTER SEVEN

Inside the small carrying crate, Lady shivered. Aunt Sarah had wasted no time in shoving Lady into the metal contraption. Then she had stormed out of the house with it and headed toward town. The crate was swinging back and forth when Aunt Sarah shoved open the door to Richland's Pet Shop and stomped inside.

Dropping the crate onto the counter, Aunt Sarah looked across at the owner, Mr. Richland. The man peered inside. Spotting Lady, he smiled kindly. "Who's this precious little angel?" he asked.

Lady finds her home on Christmas morning, when Jim
Dear gives her to his wife, Darling.

Lady is a cocker
spaniel and the
loveliest dog there
is. According to
Jim Dear, the only
creature more
perfect than Lady
is Darling.

Darling and Jim Dear love Lady very much. They've gotten her a collar to show her how important she is.

Tramp is a street dog. He has friends throughout the city and always charms his way into getting free food.

Jock is one of
Lady's best friends.
Jock's human,
Stephanie, is
always dressing
Jock in the
snappiest outfits.

Trusty is a blood-
hound and retired
police dog. He lives
next door to Lady,
and she knows she
can always count
on him.

The dogcatcher posts a warning. Stray dogs are considered dangerous and will be taken to the pound!

Peg and Bull are two of Tramp's friends. They've been caught by the dogcatcher, but Tramp helps them escape.

Lady is confused as she watches a strange dog jump over her fence and hide inside her doghouse.

Aunt Sarah comes to stay with Lady. Her cats destroy the house—but Aunt Sarah thinks it was all Lady's fault.

Aunt Sarah takes Lady to the pet store to have her fitted for a muzzle.

Lady escapes but has never been this far from home. She bumps into Tramp, and he helps Lady out of the muzzle.

Lady and Tramp enjoy dinner at Tramp's favorite restaurant. They fall in love over a plate of spaghetti and meatballs.

At the pound, Lady learns that street dogs are just like her . . . they just aren't lucky enough to have homes.

When Lady returns home, she spends time with baby Lulu. It turns out Lady loves being her sister!

Jim Dear and Darling adopt Tramp. Every dog deserves a home—and now Tramp finally has one.

Aunt Sarah let out a humph. She opened the door to the crate, and Lady gingerly stepped out.

"Her name is Lady," Aunt Sarah said. "Although I dare say it doesn't suit her."

Mr. Richland looked surprised. "No?" He made a kissy face at Lady, who wagged her tail. From his expression, she could tell he didn't agree with Aunt Sarah.

Rolling her eyes, the woman pointed at Lady's thin gray collar. "I need something to keep her from terrorizing us any longer."

Pulling his gaze from Lady, the pet shop owner reached behind the counter. He grabbed a thin harness and held it up. "A training harness?"

"She can't be trained," Aunt Sarah said.

Quickly, Mr. Richland offered several more options: obedience classes, training aids, chew toys. Each was met with a firm shake of the head from Aunt Sarah. Finally, she held up a hand, stopping him. "Don't you have anything serious in this 'establishment'? I need to stop her from acting out . . . for good."

At that, Mr. Richland's eyes narrowed. "Perhaps something—or someone—has been causing her to act out?"

Ignoring him, Aunt Sarah let her gaze travel over the wall of leashes and collars. Her eyes stopped on a wire muzzle hung low to the ground, barely visible. It was the only one of its kind, and from the dust on it, it was clear Mr. Richland had never had cause to move it—until then.

"You're sure that's necessary?"

Aunt Sarah nodded. Mr. Richland reached over and unsnapped Lady's collar. He placed it on the counter and lifted the wire muzzle. Lady began to back away. But it was no use. Before she could do anything to stop it, Mr.

Richland snapped the muzzle over her nose and clipped it to an ugly collar that wrapped tightly around her neck. Lady shook her head, the feeling of the wire on her face frightening her. As she wiggled and wormed, she moved closer to the edge of the counter. Then Lady fell to the ground.

Taking off, Lady careered around birdcages and over bags of food. She didn't stop—not even when she heard things crashing and Aunt Sarah shouting angrily. She had to get out of there. Spotting the door, she raced toward it. To her relief, it swung open as a mother and son entered the store. She slipped out and sprinted onto the street.

Lady ran and ran. The noises of the passing carriages and trolleys scared her and made her move faster. She had no idea where she was going. She had never been to that part of town. There were only a few small trees, and she didn't see any other dogs as she ran. Her heart pounding, she ducked into an alley.

Immediately, the sounds of the street faded, muffled by the high brick walls on both sides of her. Lady's pace slowed. Taking a deep breath, she let her heartbeat return to normal as she made her way farther down the alley.

Then she came to a dead end. In front of her, a large fence rose between the buildings, blocking her path. Lady checked for a way through, but there wasn't one. Sighing, she turned to head back to the street when she heard a deep, low growl.

Lady watched as a huge dog stepped out of the shadows. "Oh, thank goodness," she said happily. "I am so glad to see another dog. It is *crazy* out there." She nodded toward the street before adding, "I need some help."

The dog raised an eyebrow. "You need some help?" he asked. "For what, to steal my stash?"

Lady looked around, confused. His stash?

All she saw was a pile of leftover food and trash. "You mean this . . . garbage?" The dog let out an angry growl. Realizing she might have said the wrong thing, Lady tried to fix things. "It looks like stellar garbage. I'm just . . . not interested. Personally," she said weakly. The dog wasn't buying it. He began to stalk toward her. "I'll just go, then. . . ."

"You're not going anywhere," he growled.

Lady gulped. She ran back, farther into the alley. But the fence was blocking her path. There was no way out. She was trapped. What was she going to do now?

"Stop!"

The word echoed through the alley, surprising Lady—and the other dog. Both looked up. There, standing on a rooftop, was Tramp. His dark gray face was in shadow, and his body seemed bigger with the sun behind him.

"Don't make any sudden moves," Tramp

said. He sounded serious. "You're dealing with a killer here."

He hopped down from one fire escape to the next and landed on the ground in front of Lady.

Shooting her a look that clearly said, "Stay quiet," Tramp moved closer to the big dog. Lady lay down, putting her head on her paws. She had no idea what was going on. But Tramp was there—and for some reason, that made her feel better.

The big dog puffed up his chest, clearly pleased to be called a killer. He let out a laugh.

It died in his throat as Tramp shook his head. "I'm not talking about you, Isaac," he said. He nodded at Lady. "I'm talking about her. Don't let those floppy ears fool you." Walking closer to Isaac, he nudged him with his shoulder. "Aren't you wondering why she's wearing a *muzzle*? Why would she dare come near your stash?"

Isaac's eyes narrowed. "You know, I was wondering about that. . . ."

That was just the opening Tramp wanted. "This dog is rabid," he whispered. "You know what 'rabid' means, right?"

Isaac had no idea.

Neither did Lady. She had never heard of anyone being "rabid." Did Tramp mean "rabbit"? Was her muzzle supposed to stop her from hopping? She shot Tramp a look, begging him silently to help her understand what was going on.

"Rabies," Tramp said. He was talking to Isaac, but he kept his eyes on Lady. "You know, like when you act dangerous and contagious and scary. Like you're going to kill someone . . ."

Oh! Lady got it! She knew what Tramp was trying to do. Jumping to her feet, she made herself look as wild and scary as possible. She lifted a paw and let her tongue hang out so that it rested on the muzzle. She began to wobble around the alley. "I have rabies!" she said, to make it clear. "I am acting dangerous. And contagious."

Isaac nervously stepped back. "Easy, easy . . ." he said.

"And sometimes it's even more subtle than that," Tramp said, shooting her a look.

She was having too much fun to stop. "I have a really *real* disease," she added. Then, as Tramp groaned, she let out a strange growl.

"Ahhh!" Isaac screamed. "She's got it bad, doesn't she?"

Lady stumbled around, rubbing her fur against the brick walls of the alley and the garbage pails. "I got rabies all over your garbage!" she cried.

"Even the sausages?" Tramp said, perking up. He nodded at the stash of links.

Lady was confused—but only for a moment.

Then her eyes widened as she figured it out. She moved toward Isaac's stash of leftovers and slowly pressed herself against the food. "Oh, yes. Especially the sausages. They're contagious now!"

Isaac had moved from slight nervousness to full-blown panic. He looked at Tramp. "What do we do? What do we do?" He turned and trembled as he met Lady's gaze. "What about my stash?"

"*Go!* Just leave it, it's covered in rabies!" Tramp shouted, a glint in his eye. At the same time, Lady rushed at Isaac. The combination was too much for the big dog. Screaming, Isaac hightailed it out of the alley, leaving Lady, Tramp, and the garbage. The duo dissolved into giggles.

Tramp turned to Lady. "Well, I never thought I'd see you here," he said when he finally got his laughter under control.

"Well, I never thought I would actually be happy to see you," Lady replied.

Tramp shrugged. Moving past her, he walked to Isaac's abandoned garbage and picked up a sausage link. He bit down, letting out a happy little groan. It had been weeks since he'd had a good sausage.

"Do you think you could quit stuffing your face for one second and help me out of this muzzle?" Lady asked, moving her head up and down. "It's the least you could do, really."

Tramp lifted an eyebrow. He kept chewing for a moment. Then he swallowed. "The least *I* could do?" he repeated. "I just saved your skin."

"Well, your 'plan' wouldn't have worked without me," she pointed out. She eyed the links lying in front of Tramp's feet. "Which makes half of those sausages mine, by the way. But I'll settle for help just getting this thing off my face, please." She lifted a paw to the cold metal of the muzzle.

Tramp hesitated. Lady waited, her heart thumping. She needed his help. She didn't want to tell him why she had the muzzle or that he had been right. She just wanted to get it off. Finally, Tramp nodded.

"Okay, fine. Yeah. I think I have a friend who can help you out."

He turned and moved down the alley. Lady followed, her head low.

CHAPTER EIGHT

Entering the park at the center of the town with Lady close behind, Tramp made his way to a large bronze statue of a man holding an ax and wearing a big hat. Lady looked at Tramp. "This is your friend?" she said, nodding at the bronze frontiersman.

Tramp shook his head. "Don't be ridiculous," he said. "*This* is my friend." He pointed to a smaller bronze statue at the frontiersman's feet. It was a beaver. Its two large front teeth gleamed in the sun.

"Do you know what 'friend' means?" Lady

asked. She was seriously beginning to question her decision to follow Tramp anywhere.

Ignoring her comment, he pulled her to the statue and tried to hook the muzzle strap around the beaver. "You'll have to get a little closer," he said. Lady reluctantly moved a few steps. "There!" Tramp pulled back. Then he continued to fiddle with the strap. His nose pressed against Lady's neck, and she felt his breath on her fur.

For a moment it was quiet. The only sounds were Tramp's breathing and the scratching of the beaver's bronze teeth against the strap. After all the excitement of the morning, Lady found herself enjoying the peace.

And then Tramp went and broke it.

"So . . . not trying to be a 'told you so,' or anything," he began, "but . . . baby moves in, dog moves out?"

Lady hated that she had already had the same

thought. There was no way she was going to admit that to Tramp, though. "It's not what it looks like," she said.

"Got it, got it," he said. "Kinda looks worse to me." His words were teasing, but his tone was kind. His eyes rested on her, and Lady grew uncomfortable. This nice Tramp was unsettling.

Lady changed the subject. "I'm so glad we're doing this *after* you decided to eat garbage."

Tramp didn't bite. Instead, he carefully got his teeth between the strap and Lady's neck. Then he began to pull. He pushed back against the statue, using it for leverage. "Let me just . . ." he said, his voice muffled by the leather. He gave it several more tugs, loosening the leather with each pull. "Okay, time for the final step." Moving around, he was face to face with Lady. Their eyes locked. Behind his shaggy brows, Tramp's brown eyes grew soft.

"Uh, final step," Lady said, breaking the moment.

Startled, Tramp shook his head. "Oh, yeah, the final step," he said, snapping back to attention. "That's what I was about to do. . . ." Giving the muzzle one last tug and then a quick snip, he pulled back. The muzzle came loose, and Lady stepped out of the horrible contraption. "Wow! That actually worked!"

Laughter bubbled up inside Lady. Until then, she hadn't realized how scared she was that Tramp wouldn't be able to free her. Now that she was out of the muzzle, she couldn't stop laughing. Tramp's eyes were twinkling. He seemed as relieved as Lady felt.

The mission complete, an awkward silence fell over Lady and Tramp. She wasn't sure what to do next. She looked around the park. She had no idea where she was or how much daylight was left. But she didn't feel like she could ask Tramp for another favor. "Well, um, thanks for your help." Even as the words left her mouth, she knew they sounded weak. He had rescued her. He probably deserved more than just a thanks.

Tramp looked surprised. "Bye?"

Lady turned on her heel and set off. Every few feet she had the urge to turn around. She was about to stop and go back when she heard footfalls behind her. Then Tramp dropped into step beside her.

"You know where you're going, right?" he asked.

Lady gave Tramp a look. "I think I'm capable of finding my own way home," she said.

"Okay, nice knowing you, then," Tramp said. With a wag of his tail, he turned and headed in the opposite direction.

Fine, go, Lady thought. *I don't need you to find my way home. It's my home, after all. How hard can it be to sniff out?* But as she continued on, she realized that it was actually hard—very hard. There were dozens of smells and many people. She couldn't find any familiar landmarks. Her head began to hang lower, and her stride became less confident. She took a few steps to the right. Then to the left. She went back right. Then it hit her.

She was completely lost. Sighing, she stopped. She was really beginning to dislike that Tramp always seemed to be right.

"Wrong way."

Turning, Lady saw Tramp standing a few feet away. He had a pleased expression on his scruffy face, like he knew what she had been thinking. "I mean," he went on, "if you're going home, that would be the wrong way."

"I *know*," Lady said, rolling her eyes. "I just . . . wanted to see what was over there." She nodded toward a clump of bushes to her right. She began to move in the opposite direction.

"That's also the completely wrong way," Tramp pointed out.

Whipping around, Lady stomped her foot. "Fine," she huffed. "If you care so much, then why don't you just help me get home?" Tramp laughed, which only made Lady more annoyed. He was enjoying this!

Nodding toward another park exit, Tramp started to walk off. "Follow me, kid," he said.

Lady narrowed her eyes. True, she was going to have to rely on Tramp to get home. But that didn't mean she had to follow him. Taking off, she raced past him. She let out a laugh of her own as he barked in surprise.

She had had a terrible morning. It was time to have some fun.

Lady and Tramp ran through the streets, dodging and weaving between people's legs.

The wind whipped at Lady's ears. Fresh air filled her nose, and the sun warmed her back. It felt wonderful.

But finally, she slowed to a walk.

As her breathing also slowed, she and Tramp fell into step side by side. They walked in comfortable silence. Feeling Tramp's eyes on her, she looked at him. He was watching her curiously. "I don't want to pry or anything," he said softly, "but are you sure you *want* to go home?"

"Where else would I want to go?" she asked defensively.

Tramp shook his head. "I'm not trying to make you feel bad," he went on. "You can tell me. I'm not going to judge."

"I told you already," Lady said, picking up her pace. "This is just a big misunderstanding. I'm sure Jim Dear and Darling are worried sick about me right now."

"Sure . . ." Tramp said, clearly not buying it. He looked around at the various storefronts and nodded at a telephone pole. "I'm not seeing a lot of lost dog posters," he pointed out.

Lady frowned. Tramp could stand there and make judgments, but he didn't know anything. He said he knew people. But he didn't know *her* people. He had never even met Darling, and he had seen Jim Dear only once. He didn't know how wonderful and amazing they were. "They love me," she said. "They would never let me wind up on the streets on purpose. . . ." Her voice faded. She knew her humans wouldn't abandon her on purpose, but they *had* left her. A little bit of doubt crept in.

Shaking her head, Lady tried to push the thoughts away. She spoke again, as much to convince herself as to convince Tramp. "Home isn't just a place where I live," she said. "It's where my family is. So of course that's where I want to go."

Once more, silence fell over the pair. Lady slowly lifted her head. She met Tramp's eyes. To her surprise, he wasn't looking at her with amusement like he usually did. His eyes were serious and sad. "Well, all right," he finally said with a determined nod. "In that case, we're taking a shortcut."

CHAPTER NINE

Lady's words echoed in Tramp's head as he led her away from the center of town. She had sounded so confident even though he knew she had to be scared. All Lady had ever known was the love and safety of her home. Now she was on the streets. And for some reason, Tramp wanted to make her feel better.

Moving down an unmarked path, he sniffed. The air was beginning to smell different. They were getting closer. *Good.* He had a hunch that Lady had never been to that part of town before.

A moment later, as the wide river came

into view, sparkling in the sunlight, Lady gasped. Tramp smiled to himself. He had been right. She had definitely never been to the river before. He had to admit it was pretty impressive. It seemed to stretch on forever. The water rippled in the light breeze and reflected the clouds above.

Along the shore, several boats, including a large riverboat, were tied to a long dock. Passengers were boarding, talking and laughing as they prepared for the sunset cruise ahead. Tramp nodded toward the boat.

Lady followed his gaze. Then her eyes widened. "That's our shortcut?" she asked.

Tramp nodded. "Yep, it's easy," he said. "Just don't get caught." Taking a few steps back, he breathed in. Then he began to run toward the dock. Pushing off with his back legs, he flew through the air and landed on the boat. Looking over the water at Lady, he smiled.

"I'm not going to do that," Lady said. Then, as Tramp watched, she calmly walked up to the passenger ramp and fell into step beside a woman wearing a fancy gown and twirling a parasol. The ticket agent, spotting Lady, said a warm hello, mistaking her for the woman's dog. With a wag of her tail, Lady was on the ship.

As the huge paddle wheel began to spin, Lady made her way to the upper deck, where Tramp was standing. Below him the water was a swirl of white as the boat moved away from the shore. He lifted an eyebrow. Lady kept surprising him. For a sheltered house pet, she was quite good at making her way through unusual situations.

"Maybe next time you should ask me if I have any ideas before you risk your life unnecessarily," she said, joining him.

"Ohhh, is that your way of saying you don't want me to die?" Tramp teased.

Lady couldn't help smiling. "I didn't say that," she replied.

Tramp pretended to look offended. "So now you want me to die?"

Shaking her head, Lady looked over the water. It was peaceful on top of the riverboat. It felt nice to stop running. Suddenly, something occurred to her. "I never asked," she said. "What's your name?"

The question startled the dog. Then he shrugged. "Tramp, I guess. Truth is I don't really have a name," he answered. "People call me Buddy, or Spot, or Butch, or Hey Get Out of the Trash." He chuckled at the last one. "But who needs a name? I'm my own best friend. The sky's my roof. I walk where I want to walk. . . ."

Lady giggled. The sky was his roof? "You're funny," she said.

Tramp grinned at her. From below came the sounds of a band warming up. The entertainment for the human passengers was being readied. Gesturing for her to follow, Tramp led her closer to the edge. On the lower deck, a jazz band was taking its place. As they played their notes, Tramp barked along, wildly off-key.

"Self-taught," Tramp said when he finished. "I'm not the best technical singer. But sometimes it's not really about having soul, or depth. Sometimes it's just about—"

"Volume?" Lady finished for him. "Enthusiasm?"

Tramp looked at her, impressed. Her smile grew broader. Tilting her head back, she joined in.

As the sun began to sink below the horizon, the riverboat made its way slowly back to the dock. On the upper deck, Tramp watched the shore get closer. He realized he didn't want the cruise to end.

Turning to look at Lady, Tramp saw something new in her eyes. It looked like . . . affection. She nodded toward the dock and asked where they were going next.

Tramp couldn't believe it. He was having one of the best nights of his life. First he and Lady had danced and sung on the riverboat. Then she had followed along happily when he suggested a carriage ride through the streets. Of course, they hadn't actually been *in* the carriage. They had hitched a ride on the low back step. But they had gotten the same beautiful view of the huge live oaks, their branches heavy with moss, and had watched as the lamplighters came out to light the lamps one by one, giving the streets a golden glow.

They had sat shoulder to shoulder, enjoying the moment—and each other's company.

Seeing the wonder in Lady's eyes, Tramp bumped her. "Plenty to do out in this big ol' world," he said.

Lady nodded, a flash of sadness crossing her face. "I bet there is," she said softly.

Tramp hadn't meant to make Lady sad. All he wanted to do was make her happy. He saw that they were passing by a familiar alley. He quickly hopped off the back of the carriage. Behind him, he heard Lady shout as she scrambled after him. "How about a little warning?" she asked when she reached him. Her tone was teasing.

Raising a paw, Tramp gestured to a catwalk that ran up and over a brightly lit street. "After you," he said, pretending, for once, to play the part of a gentleman.

With a nod, Lady walked ahead. Tramp watched for a minute. There was something different about Lady. He had never liked spending much time with any other dogs. But he realized he wanted to spend all his time with her. Shaking off the thought, he caught up to her on the catwalk.

"What is all this?" she asked, nodding down at the groups of people dining at tables below.

"This?" Tramp said excitedly. "This is my favorite part of town. It's Restaurant Row!"

Lady looked confused. "Restaurant Row?" she repeated.

Tramp nodded, beaming. "They've got French, they've got Chinese. Good ol' steak and potatoes. They've got it all."

"And they just *give* it to you?" Lady asked. Then she shrugged. "Let's give it a try."

His smile broadened. Lady was in for a treat. But then he hesitated. "Don't we have to get you home?" he asked softly.

"Oh, yeah," Lady said, as if only just remembering. "Home." She looked down at the diners and then at the catwalk. She sighed and stopped walking.

Tramp cocked his head. "You okay?" he asked. "What's wrong?"

Lady's mouth opened and closed as she struggled to find the words. Tramp waited. He was getting worried. He had learned that Lady was adventurous, brave, and a bit guarded, but she was also opinionated. She had never held back. But now she was silent, lost in her thoughts. As he watched, Tramp could tell she was getting emotional.

"I'm not sure I have a home to go back to still . . ." she finally said, the admission heartbreaking for her.

Tramp stepped closer. He wasn't sure what to do. He wanted to make her feel better. But how? "Oh, hey," he said. "It's okay. . . ."

"You were right," she said, her voice shaking. "The baby moves in, and the dog moves out.

It happened . . . just the way that you said it would."

Tramp bit back a groan. He wished he had never said that. It was mean, and clearly, it had stuck with Lady. Stepping even closer, he shook his head. "I know you probably think that's what I wanted to hear, but it wasn't," he said. His voice grew thicker with emotion as he added, "Especially this time."

The faintest flicker of a smile flashed over Lady's face. But then it was gone.

Tramp couldn't let Lady stay sad. He had put that terrible thought into her head. Now he needed to find a way to get it out of there. He glanced down at the restaurants below and smiled. *Yes,* he thought. He had the perfect way to get Lady back in good spirits.

CHAPTER
TEN

Lady followed Tramp down into the alley. Dozens of different smells hit her nose, making her stomach rumble. She realized she had not eaten in a while.

Tramp stopped in front of an open door. Through it, Lady could see men and women rushing back and forth, their hands full of plates. Steam hissed, and grease sizzled on giant stoves. Suddenly, a man appeared in the doorway. He was holding a box of vegetables. Spotting Tramp, he smiled hello. But then his smile faded.

"Bad timing, Butch," he said. "We've got a full house tonight."

Lady shot Tramp a look. *Butch?* That was one of the names he had mentioned. Clearly, he came to this place often.

Turning to go inside, the man stopped, noticing Lady for the first time. He lifted an eyebrow as he looked back and forth between the dogs. Leaning down, the man gave Lady a warm pat on the head.

An angry voice called out from the kitchen. "Joe! We've got a full house!" A moment later, an older man poked his head out into the alley. Tony was the owner of the restaurant. As he spotted Joe patting Lady, his face instantly softened.

"Sorry, boss," Joe said. "It's Butch. I think he's got himself a girlfriend."

"You've gotta be kiddin' me!" Tony cried, his deep accented voice echoing in the brick alley.

Lady tensed, ready to run if she needed to. Tony looked upset, and after her experience with Aunt Sarah, she didn't want to take a chance. But then, to her surprise, Tony let out a huge laugh and crouched down on his knees. He made kissy noises as he reached out to scratch both Lady and Tramp, yelling to Joe to get the dogs some food.

Hearing footsteps, Lady saw Joe coming back out, two large bones in his hands. Her mouth watered.

"Bones?" Tony shouted, apparently not at all pleased. He shook his head. "What's the matter with you? Tonight Butch gets the best in the house." Tony got to his feet, and he and Joe jumped into action. Joe brought out a large wooden barrel. He placed it in the center of the alley, then whipped a red-and-white-checkered cloth, just like the ones on the tables in the restaurant, out of his

apron and spread it over the barrel. A menu and a candle, dripping wax, followed. He gestured to Lady and Tramp to sit.

Slowly, Lady approached the makeshift table. She had never had a dinner out before. Her stomach rumbled, this time with nerves, not hunger. Sitting down, she looked across at Tramp. As usual, he looked completely at ease as Tony walked over to take their order.

From the doorway, the older man called out to Joe. "Butch says he wants two spaghetti specials. Heavy on the meatballs!"

Tramp let out a bark of approval. Tony walked back into the kitchen to prepare the meals. Joe followed, shaking his head.

When they were gone, Lady looked at Tramp. He gave her a lopsided grin, which she returned. She had heard Darling and Jim Dear talk about their dinner dates before Lulu was born. They talked about the food, the waiters, the mood. This was just like that—sort of. Spending time with Tramp was nothing like Lady could ever have imagined. Suddenly, Tony reappeared, breaking the silence. He held a huge bowl full of spaghetti and meatballs.

"For our boy Butch and his nice new lady friend," Tony said as he placed the bowl on the table between them. *"Buon appetito."*

Lady and Tramp exchanged looks. What were they supposed to do now? Neither of them was used to this kind of treatment. Lady normally ate out of a dog bowl, and Tramp ate off the street. Shrugging, Tramp gently nudged a meatball toward Lady with his nose. Lady leaned down and gingerly bit it with her teeth. She ended up with sauce on her nose, but she didn't care. The meatball was delicious. She went in for another bite as Tony and Joe once again appeared behind her. Only this time, they were holding musical instruments. As the stars twinkled in the sky, they began to play a private concert for Lady and Tramp.

As Lady took a bite of the pasta, she smiled. She realized she was happy. With the music playing and the candle sparkling, it was warm and cozy. Pulling one strand of spaghetti into her mouth, she didn't realize Tramp was working on the same piece until their noses touched. For a moment, neither of them moved. The music played on, then she pulled back. Meeting Tramp's gaze, Lady blushed.

She wasn't sure what was happening. But one thing was certain: she was beginning to really like Tramp.

The moon was high in the sky by the time Lady and Tramp finished their dinner. She didn't say anything, but Tramp seemed to know that Lady still wasn't ready to go home. They walked slowly, enjoying the sights and sounds. They passed by a giant fountain surrounded by beautiful trees. They meandered down cobblestoned streets and up into a peaceful park. At the top of a gentle hill, Tramp came to a stop. He nodded to the whole town, spread out below them.

"Lady, the world," he said, as if introducing two new friends. "World, Lady. I think you two are going to get along just great."

Looking over the town, Lady realized she had lived there her whole life yet had never really seen it before—not until she met Tramp. As he let out a howl beside her, Lady tilted her head back and joined him. She had never done it before—and it felt incredible.

Lowering her head, she shyly met Tramp's gaze. He was smiling at her. "Look at you. Howling at the moon. Digging some music.

Enjoying a beautiful evening stroll." He paused before adding, "Yesterday the only experiences you had were behind a fence."

It *was* nice to be out. But there had been a lot of good times behind that fence, too. "I feel bad about leaving them," she said softly.

Tramp shot her a look. The moment had taken a serious turn. "They already left you," he said. "I know how much it hurts—"

Lady shook her head. "How would you know?" She stared at Tramp. She was trying to figure out what he was thinking behind his big brown eyes. Then it hit her. "Oh. You do know. You used to have a name. . . ."

Tramp nodded and told her his story. Like Lady, he had had a home and people who loved him. And then the baby arrived. Things changed—slowly at first. Just a little less love, fewer pats. And then, on a dark night, one of Tramp's humans put him in a car, drove him to the outskirts of town, took off his collar, and left him.

Just like that, Tramp went from house dog to street dog.

"I'm so sorry," Lady said when he finished. "I didn't know."

Tramp shrugged. "Eh," he said. "Every dog's got to learn sometime. You learned today: humans don't do loyalty." Lady opened her mouth to protest. But then Tramp gave her a smile, and when he spoke again, her heart melted. "And if I were with them still, I wouldn't have met you. And we wouldn't have had this amazing day."

"And night," Lady said, returning the smile.

"It doesn't have to end," Tramp said. "Every day could be an adventure. You and me. No loyalty to anyone . . ."

Lady cocked her head. "Except to each other, right?"

Tramp's eyes widened. He clearly hadn't expected Lady to say that. The words had surprised her, too. She waited for him to say something. He stood, shifting on his feet. He opened his mouth to speak and then stopped as lights flashed across the park. Turning, they both saw Elliott, the dogcatcher, clambering up the hill.

"Run!" Tramp said, already on the move. Lady stood frozen. "We gotta run—now!"

Lady didn't wait another moment. As Tramp took off, she followed. Behind them, Elliott kept chasing.

CHAPTER ELEVEN

Tramp raced across the grass. He could hear Lady's terrified breathing close behind.

At the bottom of the hill, he paused. Ahead of them was the train yard. Looking at Lady, he pointed to the long fence that ran along the yard. "We need to split up," he said. "Go that way! I'll find you!"

Lady hesitated, not wanting to leave him. Pushing her gently away from the train yard, he slipped through the fence. "Don't worry about me," he said. "I'll figure something out. I always do."

As Elliott's light swung wildly over the fence, Lady gave Tramp one last look and then took off. When he was sure she was out of sight, Tramp let out a bark. Instantly, Elliott's light was on him. *Perfect.* That was just what Tramp wanted. Bounding onto the tracks, he began to run through the yard, Elliott at his heels.

Tramp weaved in and out of the trains sitting still on the tracks. He could hear hammers banging on anvils in a nearby workshop. He ran toward the sound. After he slipped into the workshop, he rushed past workers getting ready to end their night shift. Just then, Elliott appeared. Tramp looked around. Seeing an open door, he headed toward it. But suddenly, one of the workers, finished for the night, started to shut it.

Leaping up onto a table, Tramp began to bark. The worker turned, surprised to see Tramp out so late. He held the door open just long enough for Tramp to jump through. Tramp didn't wait to see if that had stopped Elliott. He kept running. He skidded to a stop when he saw the foreman.

Tramp was trapped. If he went forward, the foreman would get him. If he went back, Elliott would surely stop him. Just when he thought he was done for, he heard barking. Distracted by the noise, the foreman turned, giving Tramp just enough time to slink through an open window of a vacant train car and out the other side.

As he raced into the open air of the train yard, Tramp let out a shout. He had gotten away—again! He did a little leap of joy. He couldn't wait to tell Lady all about his narrow escape. But then a mournful howl filled the air. Tramp stopped. As he looked up at the bridge that ran over the train yard, Tramp's heart sank.

Lady, her head back as she howled, was being shoved into Elliott's paddy wagon. She had been caught. It must have been her bark that had distracted the foreman. She had saved him—only to be caught herself.

Furious with himself, Tramp turned to go after her. But before he could make it even a dozen steps, Isaac emerged from the shadows. "I've been looking for you . . . thief."

Tramp groaned. *Not now*, he thought. "Isaac, please," he said. "I need to get by."

He moved to go around Isaac, but the big dog had other plans for Tramp. Stepping in front of him, Isaac blocked his path. Helplessly, Tramp watched as the paddy wagon drove off—with Lady inside.

Lady had never been so scared. She was in the pound.

As the doors to the pen closed, Lady pushed herself back into a corner. She shook as she looked at the odd assortment of dogs around her. Some were old, their eyes foggy, while others, like a pair of cute puppies, were young. Suddenly, the crowd of dogs parted. A small dog with long, flowing fur gracefully falling over one eye appeared. Beside her was a squat bulldog. They walked to Lady and stood right in front of her.

"Oh, just look at you," the pretty dog said in a husky voice. "Not used to digs like these, are you, honey?" Lady didn't answer.

Another pair of dogs approached, sniffing the air. "Smells like she's had a bath," one of them said bitterly.

Peg, the dog with the nice hair, shooed them away. They were just jealous, she said. Peg explained that there were two types of dogs in the pound: those who were adoptable—like

Lady—and the "others." Those were the dogs who, for whatever silly reason, people didn't think were "good" enough. They were the older dogs, or the dogs who had a droopy lip or a lazy eye. The dogs whose coats weren't shiny or whose tails didn't wag hard enough.

"But that's wrong," Lady said when Peg had finished. "Every dog should be adoptable." She thought about the night: running under the stars, howling at the moon. "Maybe I'm a street dog now, too," she added softly.

Bull, the bulldog, moved closer. "How *did* you end up here, anyway?" he asked.

"A friend and I ran into trouble and got split up. He—"

Peg cut her off. "'He'?" she repeated, suddenly more interested. "This is about to get juicy. Does he have a name?"

"He told me he doesn't have a name," Lady answered honestly.

Peg and Bull shared a look. The other dogs nodded. They all knew who Lady was talking about. Tramp was legendary—and so was his reputation of running off at the first sign of trouble. He was a charmer through and through, Peg told Lady. But more than that, he was a loner. He had a good heart, but he never opened it. Whatever they had shared out on the street, it was an illusion, Peg explained. At the end of the day, Tramp cared about only one dog—himself.

Lying down, Lady put her head on her paws. The night had been perfect. But then she remembered the moment—right before they got caught—when Tramp hesitated about their future. Maybe Peg was right.

Hearing the metal door squeaking open, Lady lifted her head. She saw Elliott. He scanned the room and then, seeing her, walked over and picked her up. She wiggled in his arms, trying to get free. She barked to the other dogs, but they could do nothing to help her.

"Lady!"

At the sound of Darling's voice, Lady's ears perked up and her fear vanished. Looking over Elliott's shoulder, she saw Jim Dear and Darling. Huge smiles broke over both their faces when they saw her. Grabbing her out of Elliott's arms, they hugged her tight.

"You must have been terrified," Darling said, rubbing her nose into Lady's neck. As she cooed, Jim Dear ushered them out of the pound. Lady glanced back over her shoulder. The last thing she saw was Peg and the others watching her go—a mixture of happiness and jealousy on their faces.

For the whole ride back to their house, Darling gave Lady belly rubs and kisses. When he could, Jim Dear reached over and scratched behind her ears, just the way she liked it. And when they finally got home, Darling insisted on carrying Lady into the house. Only when they were safely inside, with the door firmly shut behind them, did Darling let her down.

"I can't believe you were running around town all alone," Darling said as she knelt down and put Lady's collar—the one she had lost at the pet store—back on. "It's awful."

Lady let out a bark of agreement. Then she took a few prancing steps around the room. The jingling of her name tag filled her with happiness.

And then Aunt Sarah appeared.

Bending down, she tried to pet Lady. Lady backed up. She wanted nothing to do with the woman. And neither, it seemed, did Jim Dear and Darling. They didn't need Lady to tell them what had happened. They had put it together. And now they wanted Aunt Sarah gone. As they ushered her out the door, the woman paused and pointed at Lady.

"If I were you, I'd think long and hard about letting that dog get close to the baby," she said. "Next time—"

"There won't be a next time," Jim Dear said. Without another word, he nudged Sarah out the door and slammed it.

Lady let out a sigh of relief. She couldn't imagine spending another minute in the house with Aunt Sarah. And what right did she have to say Lady should stay away from the baby? She had never even met the baby, let alone done anything to her.

"You know," Darling said, looking down at Lady with a smile, "Sarah does have a point about letting you get close to the baby. . . ." Urging Lady to go with them, Jim Dear and Darling went up the stairs and into the nursery.

Nervously, Lady followed. Darling gently picked up Lulu, and then she sat on the bed, the baby between her and Jim Dear. Ever so slowly, Lady approached. Standing on her back legs, she found herself face to face with the tiny human. Lulu's eyes opened and locked on Lady. Then she let out a soft coo.

"Lulu," Jim Dear said, "this is your big sister, Lady. She's part of the family, too."

And just like that, Lady was in love.

She had been so worried that Lulu was going to take her place, but now she knew that wasn't going to happen. Jim Dear had said it himself. Lady was family, too. And from now on, she was going to take the best care of her little sister. She wasn't the center of Jim Dear and Darling's world anymore, but that was okay. At least she had a home and a family. She had seen what it was like for those dogs who didn't. And she never wanted to go back to that world.

CHAPTER TWELVE

Tramp was miserable. The days were all the same. He didn't even enjoy his morning chases with the foreman anymore, and he hadn't bothered to try to steal anything from Isaac in weeks. As he stood in the middle of a busy street market full of food, his stomach didn't even gurgle.

"What's the scam today, handsome?"

Hearing Peg's voice, Tramp looked down. The pretty dog was standing beside Bull, as usual. Tramp moved to join them, but he stopped when he saw a young man walk up to the dogs. The man held a paper bag. "The butcher's best," he said, taking two meaty bones out of the bag and tossing them to Peg and Bull.

Tramp looked back and forth, confused. What was going on? Who was this man? And who was the woman who joined him and started rubbing Bull's neck? Saying something about getting more treats, the human couple walked off, promising to be back.

And suddenly, Tramp knew exactly what was going on.

"Adopted?" he said. "You two?"

Peg and Bull nodded.

"Those two took one look at us and they had to spring us from the joint," Peg said.

Tramp's ears perked up. They had been in the joint? Maybe they had seen Lady!

"We did meet your girl," Peg answered when he asked. Bull made a few comments under his breath about Tramp's one-track mind, but Tramp ignored him. He wanted to know more about Lady. Peg didn't hold back. "You can't keep running off like that. Broke the poor girl's heart."

"She was different. We had something . . . special," Tramp admitted. "I screwed it up. I think . . . I think I might love her."

Peg and Bull cocked their heads. This was a side of Tramp they had never seen. And they liked it. It was about time Tramp let someone in. "So are you going to keep moping around here? Or are you going to go do something about that?" Peg asked.

Tramp gave Peg a mischievous smile. Then, grabbing the meaty bone out from under her, he turned to go. "I'm stealing this!" he said. With one more wag of his tail, he took off through the market.

By the time Tramp got to Lady's house, the sun had set. Bone in mouth, he sauntered into the backyard. He spotted Lady sitting inside her doghouse, her eyes on the moon.

Taking a deep breath, he stepped out of the shadows. "Hey, kid," he said softly.

Lady got to her feet. When she spotted Tramp, a smile began to cross her face. But then her expression turned cold. Tramp gulped. It was going to take some work to earn her forgiveness. He walked over and dropped the bone into the bowl by her feet.

"Now we're even," he said.

Lady eyed the bone and then looked back at Tramp. "Did you steal that one, too?" she asked.

Yup. It was definitely going to take more than a returned bone to get her back. Tramp started to tell her he had borrowed it, but then decided to go with honesty. "Okay, yes," he admitted. "I stole it." Lady frowned. "Look, back at the train yard . . . I'm so sorry for trying to split up. I should never have left your side."

Lady's eyes shone with emotion. She was listening, but her mind was somewhere else. It was as if she was thinking of someone else's words. He wondered what she had discovered about him in the pound. He thought of Peg. She could have said a few choice things to Lady. Or, knowing him, he could have botched it. "You said it yourself," she finally replied, confirming his fears. "Nobody else is loyal, so why should you be? I should have just believed you."

Her words punched at Tramp's heart. "No, you shouldn't have believed me," he said desperately. "Because being free without you there? That's just being alone." The words poured from his mouth in a rush of emotion. "Look, I know I'm a street dog and I don't have much value to anyone—"

Lady stopped him. Stepping out of her doghouse, she walked up to him. Her eyes were warm. "Don't you say that," she said. "You have value to me."

The breath he had been holding whooshed out of his lungs. He met Lady's gaze, his own eyes now full of emotion. No one had ever said anything like that to him before. His heart swelled.

"I missed you," Lady went on, making him feel even more amazing. "Sometimes I come out at night and just howl at the moon."

"We could do that again," Tramp said hopefully. "It's not too late for that, is it?"

Lady sadly shook her head. It *was* too late. She belonged here, with Jim Dear and Darling. They were her family—and she was loyal to them.

"You're right," Tramp said softly. "What you've got here, you should cherish it."

"You deserve it, too," Lady said. "You deserve love. I'm so sorry it can't be me."

The moment stretched between them. Then, inside the house, a light flicked on and Jim Dear called out Lady's name. "There's a storm coming," he said. "Come inside."

Lady looked back at Tramp. He tried to smile. "I'll go," he said. "You belong with your family." He began to make his way out of the yard. He felt Lady's eyes on him as he walked away. A part of him wanted to turn around and run back to her, beg her to let him stay. But he knew he couldn't.

As a rumble of thunder echoed in the distance, Tramp moved toward the street. He looked up at the angry clouds above. And as the drops of rain fell, his heart sank.

There was nothing left to do. He had told Lady how he felt, and she had made her decision. So what was he going to do now?

CHAPTER THIRTEEN

Lady felt horrible. The look on Tramp's face as he had walked off into the rain was heartbreaking. She hadn't wanted to say goodbye. But she couldn't leave her family, and he wouldn't leave the streets.

Slowly, she started to walk up the porch stairs. But she paused when she heard a scratching noise. Her eyes narrowed. Lowering her body, she crept up the last step. Then she began to growl. The rat! It had nearly scratched through the doggy door. At the sound of Lady's growl, it turned its beady little eyes to her. Then, with a hiss, it began to run away.

Barking furiously, Lady took off after it. She was about to get the rat when the awful little creature jumped onto the vines on the side of the house. Quickly, it began to climb up—toward the second floor and Lulu's open window.

Lady turned on her heel and scrambled back to the doggy door. She burst into the house, then raced through the kitchen and into the foyer. She headed to the stairs. But just then, Darling came down them. Stopping her, Darling turned to the door, which Lady realized was suddenly open. Elliott stood in the frame. She wriggled under Darling's hand as Elliott and Jim Dear spoke.

"The stray I'm after was running around the streets with your dog," Elliott said.

Lady growled angrily. Jim Dear bent down and patted her on the head. "Easy, girl," he said soothingly. Lady let out a bark and pulled toward the stairs. Believing her agitation was caused by Elliott's presence, Jim Dear shot the dogcatcher a look and then scooped Lady up. "I'm going to go let her calm down," he said.

Jim Dear walked back into the kitchen and put her down inside the pantry. "Just for a minute, Lady," he said gently. Then he shut the door behind her, locking her in.

Lady charged at the door and scratched helplessly at it. She needed to get out of there. Lulu was in trouble. But she was trapped. Not knowing what else to do, she began to bark desperately. She needed help.

But who was going to hear her?

Down the street, Tramp walked slowly, his heart aching. Then, over the thunder, he heard something. He paused, listening. The sound came again. It was Lady! He would recognize her bark anywhere. And she sounded terrified.

He bolted back to her house. Making his way up the back porch, he hesitated. Then he saw Lady's face at the small pantry window. Spotting him, she let out another bark.

"Help!" she shouted. "There's a rat! It's in the baby's room!"

"Where?" he asked.

"Second floor," Lady answered. "Hurry!"

Tramp took a deep breath. Going inside was about the worst idea for a dog like him. If Jim Dear or Darling spotted him, he would be in a world of trouble. But he couldn't let Lady down again. Mustering his courage, he slipped through the doggy door and made his way into the kitchen. He froze as he saw Elliott at the front door.

He took a deep breath and waited until the humans were all distracted. Then, quickly, he padded through the foyer and up the stairs.

Lady had said the second floor, but she hadn't said which room. Putting his nose to the ground, he followed the scent of baby powder to the farthest door. He peeked inside. There was the crib. Tramp tiptoed over and hopped up on his back legs to look inside. The baby was asleep, her little cheeks rosy pink, her breathing even. He let out a sigh of relief. She was okay.

Just then, a flash of lightning lit up the room. In the light, Tramp saw the rat. It was standing on top of a cabinet. It let out a hiss and then leaped—landing right on Tramp's head. Pushing back from the crib, Tramp frantically tried to shake the rat loose. He managed to get free, but as the rat fell to the floor, Tramp felt its claws digging into his head, leaving a deep scratch.

His teeth bared, Tramp backed up, putting

himself between the baby and the rat. Both in attack mode, he and the rat stood, eyes locked. And then the rat took off, racing around the room. Tramp gave chase. He sprinted after the small creature, knocking over a chair as he went. Jumping onto a table covered in toys, the rat tried to hide. But Tramp wasn't going to stop. Snarling, he leaped up, his nose pushing aside stuffed animals. Spotting what he thought was the rat, he bit down. But his teeth closed around cotton, not fur. Spitting out the toy, he watched as the rat jumped back down and headed under a dresser.

Tramp ran over and frantically swiped underneath the dresser with his paw. But the creature seemed to have disappeared. Slowly standing up, Tramp scanned the room. There was no sign of the rat. But then another flash of lightning filled the room.

In horror, Tramp saw the rat. The creature

was now perched on top of the crib. Tramp bolted across the room. But just as he reached the crib, the rat let out a hiss and jumped inside. Tramp slammed into the crib. It rocked back and forth and then began to tip over—with Lulu inside. Together, the crib and Tramp fell to the ground. The sound echoed through the house. Jumping to his feet, Tramp looked down at the baby. She was crying but unhurt.

Tramp lifted his head. His eyes narrowed as he spotted the rat clinging to a curtain right above them. If the creature jumped, it would land right on the baby. Tramp leaped at the curtain, then heard a tearing sound as he and the rat fell to the ground amid a pile of fabric. Tramp snapped, his teeth flashing. And then, suddenly, the room grew quiet. A moment later, Tramp pulled himself out from the fabric. Under the curtain, the rat was motionless.

His head pounding from the rat's claws,

Tramp stood in the middle of the room, panting. He had to tell Lady the baby was safe. But just then, the door flew open. Jim Dear and Darling let out gasps as they saw the room, now in shambles, with Lulu on the floor and a strange dog standing in the middle. Darling ran to the baby, lifted her into her arms, and began to coo gently. Jim Dear stared at Tramp.

"That's him!" Elliott shouted.

Tramp gulped. Elliott was in the doorway. He stormed over, grabbed Tramp by the neck, and began to walk him out of the room. When they reached the bottom of the stairs, Elliott looked back at Jim Dear and Darling. "You're safe now," he said, as though Tramp, not the rat, were the real problem. "We've got strict rules on what happens to dogs who hurt humans." Then he walked Tramp out of the house and shoved him into the paddy wagon.

Tramp was going to the pound. He just hoped that Lady knew he had tried.

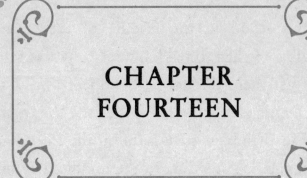

CHAPTER FOURTEEN

Lady scratched helplessly at the pantry door. She couldn't do anything but wait for someone to open it and let her out.

Finally, the door swung open. Lady bolted past Jim Dear and up the stairs to Lulu's room. She raced inside, put her nose to the ground, and began to sniff frantically. On the bed, Darling sat with Lulu.

Sniffing around the fallen furniture, Lady searched for any sign of Tramp—or the rat. Then her nose picked up something. She rushed to the curtain, now on the ground, and pushed it aside. There was the rat. Seeing its lifeless body, Darling let out a gasp.

"Oh, my goodness," she said. "Jim Dear! Come look at this!"

As Jim Dear pounded up the stairs, Lady raced down them. She flew through the doggy door and headed toward the street. Her head swiveled back and forth. Where had Tramp gone?

Hearing footsteps, she turned, hoping to see Tramp. But it was just Jock and Trusty. "Where'd he go?" she asked, hoping they knew.

Luckily, they did. "Dogcatcher took him to the pokey," Trusty said. "What happened?"

"It was the rat!" Lady cried. Then she began to run down the street. Behind her, Jock and Trusty exchanged looks. They had been quick to judge Tramp. Maybe they had been wrong. They took off after Lady.

As the trio ran down the street, Lady kept her eyes forward and her nose up. She heard Jim Dear's Model T engine rev somewhere behind her. Approaching a T-intersection, Lady looked back and forth. "Which way did they go?" she asked. There was no sign of the paddy wagon, and she couldn't smell anything.

"We'll need to sniff it out," Jock said, shivering slightly in the night air. She had lost her kilt during the run and looked, for once, like a normal dog.

"Good idea," Trusty agreed. Feeling the other dogs' eyes on him, he realized that they meant *he* should do the sniffing. "Right, of course. Leave it to ol' reliable here."

Putting his nose to the ground, Trusty began to work. He followed a scent—straight to a bench and a pair of sailors sharing a drink. That wasn't it. He put his nose back down and followed it again—this time to a pallet of

fish. Still not it. Behind him, Lady and Jock followed, growing disheartened. And then, through the other smells, Trusty caught it— the smell of Tramp! He bayed loudly and took off. "This way!" he shouted over his shoulder.

As they rounded a corner, Lady let out a happy yelp. There, up ahead, was the paddy wagon. It was making its way slowly down the street.

The paddy wagon turned another corner by the park. Lady knew where they were. She began to run through the park. Behind her ran the others.

Bursting onto the street on the opposite side of the park, Lady found herself right behind the paddy wagon. Looking up, she saw Tramp staring back at her through the bars. "We're coming!" she called. Then she began to bark frantically.

At the sound, Elliott turned. He shifted

slightly on his seat. In front of him, the horses began to move faster. Lady didn't think; she just acted. She raced to the front of the paddy wagon and threw herself in front of the horses. With frightened whinnies, they reared up. There was the sound of cracking wood as their yoke broke, and then they were free, racing off down the street. Behind them, the paddy wagon let out a groan as its front wheels, no longer supported, shattered. The paddy wagon flipped end over end. Elliott and Tramp went flying.

And then there was silence.

Lady looked around. Where was Tramp? She spun in a circle. But all she could see were the remains of the paddy wagon, and all she could hear was the distant neighing of the horses.

Then she stopped. Jock and Trusty were standing by the sidewalk, looking at the ground. Lady ran over and let out a gasp. It was Tramp! He lay on his side, his chest still beneath his dark fur. Lady felt her stomach drop. She was too late. Lifting her head, she let out a mournful howl. The eerie sound pierced the night air.

"What took you so long, kid?"

Lady stopped howling. Looking down, she saw Tramp gazing up at her, a smile on his rugged face. She smiled back. Then, as Trusty and Jock watched, she leaned down and began to nuzzle him.

"Lady!"

Hearing Jim Dear's voice, Lady lifted her head. He and Darling were making their way through the wreckage of the crash. Darling clutched Lulu in her arms.

"Thank goodness you're okay," Jim Dear said when he reached her side. He began to pet her head, and Lady leaned into his hand.

Beside her, Tramp was still and quiet, not wanting to ruin the moment.

But then, suddenly, Elliott appeared. Leash in hand, he clipped it to Tramp and yanked him to his feet. "You're still coming with me," he said. He began to drag Tramp, limping, back down the street. "I'll walk you to the pound if I have to."

Lady watched, her eyes wide with panic. She had just gotten Tramp back. She couldn't lose him again. She barked, turning her head back and forth between Tramp and Darling and Jim Dear. Behind her, Jock and Trusty joined in.

Darling looked down at her sweet dog and then at the rough-and-tumble mutt limping down the street. Suddenly, her eyes widened in understanding. "Hold on!" she cried. She handed Lulu to Jim Dear and ran to Elliott.

"You can't do this," she said when she reached the dogcatcher.

Elliott raised an eyebrow. "I not only can," he replied, "it's my duty."

Darling shook her head. She pointed at Tramp. "He was protecting our baby!"

The dogcatcher was unmoved. "The law clearly states that any unlicensed dog without a home will be immediately impounded," he said, pointing to Tramp's bare neck. No license.

"But he has a home," Darling said. Her voice was soft. But as she went on, it grew stronger. She knew in her heart that somehow this dog had been the one to save her baby. She wasn't going to let him go to the pound—not when she could do something about it. "He has a home," she repeated.

Jim Dear joined her. Putting a hand on her shoulder, he looked at Elliott. "That's our dog, sir."

Elliott looked back and forth between the husband and wife, confused. Then, slowly, it seemed to come to him. Sighing, he handed the leash over. Without another word, he walked toward the paddy wagon.

Darling looked down at the scruffy dog. His eyes were guarded. His tail was tucked between his legs. Lady went to stand beside Darling. She let out a soft whine. Slowly, his tail lifted, and then he began to hobble toward them. Reaching Lady, he lowered his head. As the pair snuggled, tears filled Darling's eyes.

It looked like their family had just grown by one more.

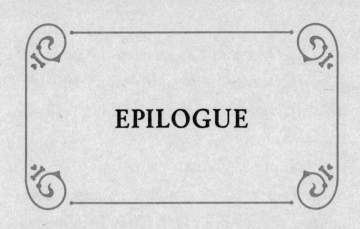

EPILOGUE

Snow once again covered the porch of Lady's house and drifted softly through the air. In the backyard, Jock and Trusty stood, looking pleased. Jock was once again dressed—this time in a snowsuit. Her adventure sans an outfit had been invigorating, but she had realized she enjoyed the comfort of clothes more—especially now that she was a big sister.

Lifting a heavy brow, Trusty looked at Jock. "I didn't know you got new recruits," he said.

Jock nodded. "My 'gift' from Stephanie," she said. Her human had been inspired by Darling and Jim Dear and had gone to the pound the very next day. Jock wouldn't admit it, but she liked having the pups around. It made the house livelier.

"Hey, pups," Trusty called out. "I'm your uncle Trusty." Immediately, the puppies were on top of the big old hound. Laughing, he settled down on the ground. "Gather round, cadets," he began, happy to have a new audience for his stories. "Wanna hear about the time I chased down a dogcatcher? Saved a poor stray with a heart of gold?"

As the pups let out yips of "yes" and tugged playfully at Trusty's long ears, Jock smiled. Things were definitely changing in the neighborhood. But she was glad they were. She looked into the window of Lady's house.

Inside, Lady sat beside the fire. The crackling logs warmed her back. Presents filled the room, and Lulu crawled her way between them, tugging at bows and already ripped wrapping.

Lady turned to look at Tramp. His coat had been washed and cleaned. The long hair around his face and eyes had been trimmed, so she could clearly see his deep brown eyes twinkling as he met her gaze. His leg, still in a sling from the paddy wagon accident, was healing. She smiled as Jim Dear knelt down next to them.

"Okay, boy," he said, "it's time we made you official."

Leaning over, he opened a small box. Inside was a collar of Tramp's very own. Gently, Jim Dear placed it around Tramp's neck. He gave Tramp a pat and then, standing back up, went to join Darling and Lulu on the couch.

"So how does it feel?" Lady asked Tramp quietly, nodding at the collar.

"You know, it kind of feels . . ." He stopped

and moved his neck this way and that, as though he wasn't sure how to describe it.

"Too tight? Too itchy?" Lady suggested.

Tramp shook his head. "I was going to say . . . it kind of feels like home."

He grinned at Lady, and she grinned right back. The lovable mutt who had thought he only belonged on the street now sat by a warm fire, with a family beside him. It was like Lady had said at the pound: every dog deserved a home, no matter what they looked like or how old they were. And now Tramp had a home of his own—with her.

As snow fell outside and music began to play, Lady and Tramp lifted their heads and barked along in harmony.